# TICK, TOCK, MYSTERY CLOCK

A RIGHT ROYAL COZY INVESTIGATION MYSTERY

HELEN GOLDEN

## ALSO BY HELEN GOLDEN

**A Right Royal Cozy Investigation Series**

*Tick, Tock, Mystery Clock (Novelette)*

*Spruced Up For Murder*

*For Richer, For Deader*

*Not Mushroom For Death*

*An Early Death (Prequel)*

*Deadly New Year (Novelette included in Vol 1 of the Riddles, Resolutions and Revenge cozy anthology)*

*A Dead Herring*

*I Spy With My Little Die*

*A Cocktail To Die For*

*Dying To Bake*

This is a work of fiction. Names, characters, places, and incidents are the product of the author's imagination, or she has used them fictitiously. Any resemblance to actual persons, living or dead, events, or locales is entirely coincidental.



ISBN (P) 978-1-915747-18-1

Edited by Marina Grout at Writing Evolution

Published by Drew Bradley Press

Cover design by Helen Drew-Bradley

First edition September 2022

# NOTE FROM THE AUTHOR

I am a British author and this book has been written using British English. So if you are from somewhere other than the UK, you may find some words spelt differently to how you would spell them. In most cases this is British English, not a spelling mistake. We also have different punctuation rules in the UK.

However if you find any other errors I would be grateful if you would please contact me helen@helengoldenauthor.co.uk and let me know so I can correct them. Thank you.

For your reference I have included a list of characters in the order they appear and you can find this at the back of the book.

# INTRODUCTION - NOVEMBER 2021

The author sat staring at her laptop screen, a look of horror creeping over her face as the reality of what she had heard dawned on her.

"So to summarise, a reader magnet is an essential tool in building a relationship with your reader. Thank you for attending this webinar. If you'd like to ask questions, please do so by using the chat button now. I will spend the next fifteen minutes answering as many of them as I can."

The author selected the chat button and typed: *Just so I'm clear, having spent months writing a book that I haven't even released yet, you now want me to write another book, and give it away for free?*

She waited. She took a sip of her tea; yuck, it was cold. Rising, she put the kettle on.

"We have a question from Helen."

The author ran back to her laptop as the course leader read her question aloud.

"Well, Helen, I understand it may seem daunting so soon after finishing your first book, but yes, you need to write something that's only available to potential readers who sign up to join your author group, and you need to give it to them for free. As I've explained, it is so you can introduce yourself to them, to let them see your style of writing and hopefully to make them want to read more from you." She smiled. "Thank you for your question, Helen, and good luck."

Letting out an enormous sigh, the author closed the lid of her laptop and stared out of the caravan window. A pink petal threw itself off the untidy rose bush at the side of the driveway. *I know how you feel*, she thought as she poured hot water over the tea bag in her cup. Standing, she opened a cupboard and took out a family-size bag of cheese and onion crisps. Grabbing a handful, she stuffed them into her mouth.

---

Her hands propping up her face, the author stared out of the window of her caravan and contemplated what she was going to write.

It had been her intention to work in the lovely new office recently built as an extension of the house. But she had to share the space with her husband, who, thanks to the recent pandemic, now worked from home. The author loved her husband dearly, but he was incapable of explaining to his colleagues how engineering stuff worked without shouting and waving his arms about. A lot.

That wasn't an environment conducive to someone who was trying to write a novel when they needed *total* quiet. So, not being the one who required a set up resembling mission control to do their job (*why do you need three screens, darling?*), the author had somewhat reluctantly volunteered to find another space to work.

Like in their caravan, which was currently parked on their drive.

On her right was a green metal shed, which housed her husband's motorbike. But if she leaned her head further around until it rested against the window, she could see the striking village church diagonally opposite their house. Parts of the church went back to the twelfth century. It was beautiful. Through the large front windows, trees and bushes lined the driveway and spilled into her neighbour's garden. On the left was the front door of their house. Sometimes the author liked to jump out at unsuspecting delivery men and give them a bit of a fright.

As she continued gazing out of the window, the author spotted one of their cats. Louie, a beautiful red-striped male Bengal, was grooming himself in the sun on her opposite neighbour's lawn. Drumming her fingers on the table, the author looked ahead of her at the two sofas, where three dogs were sprawled.

Margot, a small female chorkie, was curled into a tight ball. So cute that everyone picked her up and kissed her, she was affectionately known as 'diseased dog'. Next to her was Alfie, a large long-haired male chihuahua, who was obsessed with food and recently had been described by the vet as 'too chunky'. Opposite them, snoring loudly, was Bourbon, a hefty male black pug belonging to her niece. Like a lovable bull in a china shop, when awake, he barged around the house, leaving a trail of destruction behind him.

*I'm not procrastinating*, she told herself. She was simply waiting for inspiration.

She wondered where Fluff, a small grey long-haired female Bengal, was. The author's husband described the cat as 'an evil ball of fluff' because of her habit of peeing on his shoes. Not hearing the familiar cry of Fluff outside, a demand that the author had to stop working and let her in the front door of the house, the author cleared her throat and focused back on what she'd been told in the webinar.

The smiley lady on her screen had suggested writing a short story and using it to introduce some characters featured in her series. *Okay*, the author thought, *let's try that*.

---

*Tick, Tock, Mystery Clock* takes place seven years before *Spruced up for Murder*, the first in the *A Right Royal Cozy Investigation* series. Here we meet Perry Juke — a twenty-six-year-old head tour guide, and Simon Lattimore — a detective sergeant with Fenshire CID. When a Cartier mystery clock is stolen from Francis Court, they must work together to retrieve it.

# 1

## EARLY, SATURDAY 8 JUNE

*How did that happen?* Perry Juke plucked a pair of black nitrile gloves from his blazer pocket and snapped them on.

Hardly daring to breathe, he leaned over the walnut tiered table in front of the elaborate marble fireplace in the Green Drawing Room of Francis Court. He reached across a small black vase and a masked dancer figurine and carefully rearranged the 1924 art deco antique sterling silver frame sitting awkwardly at the back. Inside it was a black and white photograph of Evelyn, the wife of the fourteenth Duke of Arnwall, and he thought, not for the first time, how odd it was that someone had picked such an unflattering photo of her ladyship to put on display. She looked like a grumpy old man. But even so, she deserved to be straightened up so visitors could see her in her full cantankerous glory.

*Oh my giddy aunt!*

He froze, not daring to move a muscle after his knuckles brushed the exquisite Cartier mystery clock sitting behind the frame. Although the nephrite jade plinth gave it a heavy and sturdy base, a good accidental knock could send it crashing to the floor, destroying a valuable, irreplaceable piece.

His pulse racing, he leaned in even further over the table to take a closer look. The green base looked dull to him. *That's strange. It was shiny only a couple of days ago when I put it back on display...*

He shook his head. *It's probably just the light making it look like that*. Stretching his hand delicately behind the photo frame, he moved the clock back into place. He gasped. It was light. Lighter than it should be. His mouth fell open. Something was wrong.

# 2

# ONE DAY EARLIER. A FEW MINUTES BEFORE 6 PM, FRIDAY 7 JUNE

Perry poked his head around the corner of his boss' office. Alistair Barnett, a stout man with thinning hair, paced in front of his desk, glanced at his watch, and sighed. Perry cleared his throat. His boss looked up, frowning as if the last thing he'd expected to see was his head tour guide standing in the doorway.

"Mr Juke, I thought you'd be gone by now."

Perry lifted his chin. "I've finished my last checks and locked the state rooms. I thought *you* would be gone by now."

Barnett moved round his desk, opened the top drawer, and swept a small set of keys into it. "Yes, well, I'll go soon. I had a few last-minute jobs to attend to." He raised his head, his eyes squinting. Hastily withdrawing a large white handkerchief from his trouser pocket, he sneezed into it.

"Bless you," Perry responded automatically. "Are you sure you should've come back to work today, Mr Barnett? You still don't sound well. Will you be able to drive all the way to Wales?"

Barnett folded the handkerchief and wiped his nose before returning it to his pocket. "Yes, yes. Actually, I'm a lot better, thank you." Barnett's lined face was red and puffy. His hands shook.

*You don't look it*, Perry thought. But having worked for the man for nine months now, he knew there was no point in saying anything further.

"Well, I hope it goes well at your daughter's wedding tomorrow. From the forecast, it looks like it should be sunny all day."

"Thank you, Mr Juke," Barnett mumbled as he stepped round to the back of his desk and removed something from the top drawer. "I really must go up to the flat and pack, then get on the road." Looking up at Perry, he straightened and walking back towards him, reached over and grabbed a small brown leather bag that had been resting by the side of his desk. "And no doubt you want to get home. I'll walk out with you."

Barnett locked his office door, and they strolled along the corridor in silence. Passing through the magnificent Painted Hall of Francis Court, they exited by the north side door. As they reached the bottom of the terrace steps, Barnett turned to Perry. "Have a good weekend, Mr Juke. I'll see you on Tuesday."

"Enjoy the wedding, Mr Barnett," Perry replied.

# 3

## 8:20 AM, SATURDAY 8 JUNE

"Good morning, Mr Juke. You're early for a Saturday."

Perry smiled at the security officer leaning out of the window as he approached the north side gate of Francis Court. When he pushed the metal door, it clicked, its lock releasing.

"I have to do some training with one of my new guides this morning, Frank. It's best to do it early, before the public arrives."

Frank nodded. "Well, you have a good day, Mr Juke."

"You too, Frank."

He continued along the gravel path towards the main house, his hand rising to shield his eyes when he came out from the shadow of the trees and crossed the tarmac road. He pulled a pair of sunglasses out of his blazer's top pocket and put them on. Although Perry had worked at Francis Court since he was seventeen, his early morning glimpse of the magnificent Palladian-style mansion never ceased to make him smile.

Heading towards the side entrance, Perry scampered up the stone steps of the north terrace and pushed open the door, pleased to find that it had already been unlocked. Removing his sunglasses with one hand, he caught the door with his other just in time to stop it from slamming behind him. He briskly crossed the black and white chequered floor of the Painted Hall, towards an open door at the far right-hand corner that led to the Breakfast Room.

The smell of freshly brewed coffee and toasted bread gave him a warm and fuzzy feeling as he entered the restaurant and headed towards the serving counter at the opposite end.

"Good morning, Perry. Are you having breakfast?" the small lady behind the counter asked.

"Not today, Flo. I need to get straight to my office. Just a coffee to go, please, and a pain au chocolat if you have any."

She nodded and turned her back to grab a large pot of coffee from the warmer.

"How are you not the size of a house?" a feminine voice behind him teased. "You should be, you know, with all the pastries you eat."

Perry turned and stuck his tongue out at the dainty woman. "I'll have you know, Claire, that I walk on average five miles a day doing this job. I'll have walked it off before you've even started your computer."

She grinned. "Are you training the new chap this morning?"

Perry nodded. "Yes. I'm hoping he's a bit more confident on this third run through. I'd hate to extend his probation any further."

"I'm sure he'll be fine. I think you make him nervous."

"What, me?" Raising his hand to his chest, Perry leaned back and looked at her in mock surprise. "But I'm a pussycat compared to old Barnett."

"Maybe. But that's like saying Simon Cowell is a pussycat compared to Gordon Ramsey."

Perry snorted, and they both laughed.

"Here you go, Perry. One large latte and a pain au chocolat."

"Thanks, Flo, have a good day." He turned to Claire. "Lunch, one o'clock?"

She nodded, and with an air kiss vaguely aimed at her head, Perry strolled from the restaurant.

---

There was a satisfying *clunk* as Perry unlocked the door to the Green Drawing Room, the first in the ten connected rooms making up the state apartments in the east wing of Francis Court. As he pushed open the heavy wooden door, he surveyed the room before him. It was his favourite of all the staterooms, mainly because it had some more modern art déco pieces intertwined with the older ones. Evelyn, the wife of the fourteenth Duke, had used the room until her death in 1984. She had been quite a collector in her time, her most treasured pieces now scattered around the seating area in front of the dominant marble fireplace.

*Now, which items shall I test Colin on?* Scanning the area beyond the red rope, he tried to remember what he had asked the man last time. And that's when he noticed it. The silver-framed photo of Evelyn was askew.

*How did that happen?* Perry Juke plucked a pair of black nitrile gloves from his blazer pocket and snapped them on.

# 4

## 8:40 AM, SATURDAY 8 JUNE

His hand flying to his chest, his heart raced. Perry took a deep breath, steadying himself, and gingerly picked up Evelyn's pride and joy — the rock crystal and diamond Model A mystery clock made by Cartier. He loved the clock. Its delicate diamond-set arrowed hands looked almost as if they were floating in space inside the casing. He had handled it only the day before yesterday when it had come back from cleaning, and it had been a lot heavier than it was now.

The clock in his hand was not the real mystery clock.

His mouth dry, he placed it down safely on the table and stepped away. Removing his gloves, he backed up towards the door and left the room, locking it behind him.

With his back resting against the huge wooden door, he stared up at the bottom of the stone balcony above his head, his mind in a whirl.

*Think, Perry! You must tell someone.*

He straightened up, pulled down the front of his waistcoat, and breathed out with a puff.

*Mr Barnett. I must tell Barnett.*

Reminding himself that running would be inappropriate in

the Painted Hall, he moved with as much dignity as he could muster. Crossing the hall, he entered the door opposite in record time. It was only then that it dawned on him that Barnett was currently somewhere in Wales, no doubt having a hearty breakfast to prepare for his daughter's wedding later that day.

*Oh my giddy aunt. Who do I tell now?* Stopping halfway down the corridor, he swivelled a full three hundred and sixty degrees. *Lady Sarah. I will have to tell Lady Sarah.*

---

"Was the door locked when you arrived first thing? Was the alarm on? Did you notice if anything else had been moved?" Lady Sarah Rosdale, daughter of Her Royal Highness Princess Helen and Charles Astley, sixteenth Duke of Arnwall, fired questions at Perry as they hurried up the stone steps of the south terrace and into the Painted Hall.

"Yes, it was. I didn't look. Not that I could see, my lady."

Taking out his keys, Perry opened the door to the Green Drawing Room. As Lady Sarah swept past him, Perry couldn't help but be impressed by her ability to move so quickly in her sky-high Louboutin patent leather black shoes.

He pointed to the walnut tiered table. "I put it back on the table as soon as I realised."

Lady Sarah bounded across to the red rope barrier and stepped over it.

"Stop!" Tugging out a pair of gloves, he rushed towards her. "You need to wear these if you're going to handle anything, my lady."

She stopped and pivoted around. *Even in circumstances like these, she looks the epitome of elegance*, Perry thought as he handed them to her.

Taking the gloves from him, she said, “Thank you.”

Perry watched, heart in his throat, as she bent over and carefully picked up the clock.

“You’re right, Perry. This isn’t great grandmama’s mystery clock. It’s too light, the jade is dull, and the hands are not gliding. They’re jerking, see?”

Leaning forward, he looked over her shoulder. He could see the small hand juddering as it moved around the diamond-encrusted face.

“I think we need Marcus Crawley to examine it. But I agree with you. This is a fake.”

# 5

# 9 AM, SATURDAY 8 JUNE

"Thank you for coming so promptly, Mr Crawley. Mr Juke and I have concerns regarding Lady Evelyn's Cartier mystery clock. Would you be so kind as to have a look at it for me?"

After patting her chignon of dark-brown hair, Lady Sarah indicated for the curator to join them by the walnut table in the Green Drawing Room. Francis Court's expert in antiques bowed his head to her and then smiled at Perry while shuffling towards them.

Perry instinctively wanted to offer the frail, stooped man his arm, but he stopped himself. He knew from Claire, who worked in Human Resources, that Mr Crawley was only sixty-three. He looked much older. *Not surprising*, Perry thought, as he studied the pale lined face of the man heading towards them. As far as he knew, Mr Crawley spent most of his time inside his workshop hunched over objects with one eye closed, his eye loupe protruding from the other. When not at work, he disappeared to his flat in the Old Stable Block and rarely accepted invitations to socialise with the staff. He was, however, a very well-respected member of the Francis Court household, having been the curator here for forever, and Lady Sarah clearly valued his opinion.

When Mr Crawley retrieved a pair of gloves from the side pocket of his dark-blue jacket, Perry expected him to grab the clock and examine it straight away. But he didn't. Instead, he leaned forward slowly, stopping only when he was eye level with the object (*and not a moment too soon*, Perry thought, convinced he would topple over at any minute) and stared for some time at the clock.

Beside him, Lady Sarah, smoothing down her fitted green Max Mara sheath dress, sighed and looked over to Perry, her beautifully shaped eyebrows raised. Perry shook his head and shrugged. *I've no idea.*

With a movement resembling that of a claw in an amusement arcade, Mr Crawley straightened up and, keeping his body stiff, reached over the other objects with his left hand. He plucked the delicate clock off the table, then gently placed it in his other hand, moving it up and down as if assessing the item's weight. Next, he peered at the plinth the clock was attached to and moved it around in the light.

Lady Sarah looked down at the floor, massaging her temples as they waited.

"Well, my lady."

Startled when the wispy man finally spoke, Perry looked at him in surprise. His voice was much stronger than his frame suggested.

"It's strange indeed." Mr Crawley slowly shook his head. "It feels lighter than it should, and the hands are not moving in the way I would expect them to. I'm sorry to say it, but I think it's likely that this isn't the original clock. However, it's hard to do a full assessment in this room." He waved his hand towards the window. "The light is too bright for my eyes.

With your permission, my lady, I would like to take it to my workshop and examine it there in greater detail."

Perry coughed, causing Lady Sarah to turn towards him. "Shouldn't we leave it where it is, my lady, and call the police?"

She sighed, then nodded. "I'm afraid Mr Juke is right, Mr Crawley. I need to consider the next steps. Thank you for your help. And may I ask you not to discuss our suspicions with anyone else at this stage, please?"

He nodded and left the room.

"I'm not sure about this, Perry. A police investigation will no doubt attract the wrong sort of attention for us. I would hate for this incident to get into the press." She lifted her chin towards the door. "And Mr Crawley didn't actually say it's a fake. Maybe we've made a mistake?"

Perry shook his head. "Mr Crawley is, by nature, a cautious man and he won't make a final pronouncement until he's done a thorough examination on his own terms. But you could tell from his face that he knows it's not the original. I'm sorry, Lady Sarah, but I handled the real clock only a few days ago and I know that this"—he waved his hand at the clock on the walnut table—"isn't the same one."

Lady Sarah's shoulders slumped.

"Can I make a suggestion, my lady?"

Straightening up, she tilted her head to one side. "Please do, Perry."

"Why not ring Mr Anderson? He has contacts at Fenshire CID and may suggest a way of doing this low-key."

For the first time since he had burst into her office earlier this morning, a smile spread across Lady Sarah's face. "That's a splendid idea, Perry. I'll call Anderson now. Then let's go grab a coffee from the restaurant, shall we?"

---

Perry couldn't stop smiling to himself as he and Lady Sarah left the Breakfast Room on their way to meet Jack Anderson, Francis Court's head of security. *I, Perry Juke, was just seen in the restaurant having a coffee and a chat with a member of the royal family. Claire will be so jealous!* He couldn't wait to see her at lunchtime and tell her all about his new bestie who was sixteenth in line to the British throne.

As they entered the Painted Hall, the sound of a purposeful stride echoed towards them. Anderson, a stocky man in his late fifties with short black hair and a Charlie Chaplin moustache, raised his hand towards them. They all met outside the Green Drawing Room door.

"My lady." He bowed his head at Lady Sarah. "Shall we go in? I assume you have a key, Mr Juke?"

Perry nodded and opened the door, standing aside to allow Lady Sarah to go in first.

"So…" Anderson closed the door behind them. "You believe someone has stolen a valuable clock belonging to the late Duchess of Arnwall and replaced it with a fake? Is that true?"

"Yes." Lady Sarah moved towards the table which held the clock. "Perry noticed first thing this morning that someone had disturbed the picture of Lady Evelyn and while rearranging it, he moved the Cartier clock and realised that something was wrong with it."

Anderson turned to Perry, his eyebrows raised.

"I actually knocked it by mistake and it moved too easily, Mr Anderson. The original has a solid nephrite plinth, which is very heavy. Merely knocking it like I did shouldn't have caused it to move. When I picked it up, I noticed it was too light. That's when I contacted Lady Sarah."

"Thank you, Mr Juke. So you're familiar with the original item are you?"

"Yes. It's one we point out to visitors when we tour this room. The story of its presentation in 1932 to Lady Evelyn by Queen Alice as an engagement present always goes down well."

Lady Sarah smiled, glancing at the photograph of her ancestor. "It was one of her most prized possessions."

"And when do you think you last saw the original, Mr Juke?"

"It came back from Cartier on Thursday after its annual clean. Mr Barnett is normally the one to put it back on display, but as he was off sick, I did. I placed it on the table, just there, where it had been before. I assure you this one isn't the same one I handled."

Nodding, Anderson said, "So the only time someone could have swapped the clocks over would have been within the last forty-eight hours?"

"I suppose so." Perry frowned. "Although the picture was in place last night when I locked up and it was out of place when I unlocked the room this morning. I think that's when it must have happened."

Anderson turned to Lady Sarah. "If Mr Juke is correct, and it happened after we were closed to the public, then—"

Lady Sarah finished his sentence for him, "Then it must have been stolen by a member of the household."

## 6

## 10:45 AM, SATURDAY 8 JUNE

"They are sending a detective sergeant called Simon Lattimore. After I speak to him, Anderson will bring him to you. I want you to look after him and help him where you can, Perry. We're very lucky we've been able to keep this under the guise of a security review. But make no mistake, if this is not resolved soon then the investigation will be ramped up, and at that point it will be hard to keep it under wraps. I'm relying on you, Perry."

*No pressure then!* Perry took a deep breath to steady his nerves. "Yes, Lady Sarah, I'll do my absolute best."

"Thank you, Perry. Please keep me informed."

Putting down his phone on the large leather-covered desk top, he raked his hands through his pristinely styled blond hair.

*Oh no!* He immediately jumped up and legged it to the mirror behind the door of his office *Why did I do that just before I'm expecting a visitor?* Teasing his hair back into its impeccable form, he returned to his desk. Staring down at the list in front of him, he picked up a pen and started ticking off the items on his checklist.

- Cancel Colin's walk-through — tick
- Rearrange rota to cover me — tick
- Cancel public ticket tours until eleven-thirty — tick
- Cancel lunch with Claire — tick

He sighed. That had been the most frustrating one so far. How could he show off his newly found relationship with Lady Sarah if he wasn't able to tell Claire all about it?

At the knock on his door, Perry turned the list over. "Come in." He stood up straight, wanting to create the right impression for the DS from Fenshire CID.

The door opened and in walked Jack Anderson, followed by an Adonis in a bottle-green polo shirt and black jeans. Rooted to the spot, Perry stared in admiration, his mouth partly open. The man smiled at him, making Perry's body temperature rise and his skin tingle. *Oh my giddy aunt, he's gorgeous!* He wanted to smile back, but his face wouldn't co-operate. *I must look like a real dimwit, just standing here, gawping.*

Anderson coughed, and Perry dragged his attention away from the other man. Heat spread up his neck. *Get a grip, you idiot!*

"Mr Juke, this is Detective Sergeant Lattimore from Fenshire CID."

The man leaned around Anderson and held out his hand. "Call me Simon, please."

"Perry." Perry returned the firm handshake. He liked a firm handshake. *Stop it!*

"DS Lattimore has kindly offered to undertake a low-profile investigation into our mystery clock mystery." Anderson chuckled to himself. "I like that," he murmured. "I'm going to leave him in your capable hands." He turned back to Simon. "Give me a shout if you need anything, sergeant." And with that, he walked out of the room.

"I didn't really offer." Simon grinned as he walked towards the desk and sat down in the chair in front of it. Perry flicked his tongue out to lick his dry lips. "More like I was told by my inspector that I would be doing her a personal favour if I came here to help out her old boss, Anderson."

Trance-like, Perry lowered himself into the chair opposite the young DS. Resisting the urge to reach out and lightly touch the square jaw of the man in front of him, he examined the slightly tanned face further. He frowned. "Have we met before?"

"I don't think so," Simon replied, still smiling. A smile that looked familiar to Perry…

*Got it!* "Were you here during the investigation into the Earl of Rossex's death?"

A splash of red coloured Simon's cheeks. "Um, yes. Just for a few days."

There was a slightly awkward silence, then Perry smiled. "You look familiar, that's all. I must have seen you around then." He wouldn't remind Simon of their meeting — if you could call it that. It was seven years ago, after all. It's unlikely he'd remember, and even if he did, it might embarrass him to recall the incident. *Best leave it.*

"Anyway, thank you for being emotionally blackmailed into helping us. As Lady Sarah has probably already explained, we're trying to keep it quiet while we figure out what happened. Would you like to see the item in question? Well, the fake one, anyway. The room will open to the public soon, so we'll need to be quick." Aware that he was babbling, Perry jumped up. Grabbing a set of keys from his top drawer, he led Simon Lattimore to the Green Drawing Room of Francis Court.

---

"Mr Anderson said that each room in the state apartments has an alarm system that will go off if someone removed an item. Is that correct?"

"Yes. Each doorway has an alarmed surround." Perry pointed up as they walked through it. "We tag all objects and pieces of furniture, a bit like in a shop. Except our tags are very discreet. If a tagged item passes through it, it sets off a silent alarm with security. It also beeps in the vicinity, too."

Simon nodded.

Perry's gaze followed Simon as he moved around the room. He was a few inches shorter than Perry's six foot one, and he had the stocky build of someone who worked out — not to show off but to keep fit. Having never been to a gym in his life, Perry shuddered at the thought of getting hot and sweaty without having some fun to compensate. Much to Claire's annoyance, he was blessed with a body that stayed slim despite what he ate.

Crouched in front of the roped off area, Simon examined the floor. He turned on the spot, his eyes downcast. Then he looked up and their eyes met briefly. *I could get lost in those brown eyes.* Swallowing, Perry quickly looked away.

Simon straightened up and hopped over the red rope. "Can you show me the clock, please?"

Perry scuttled over.

"Is it valuable?" Simon leaned in and took a photo of the table setup. "The real one, I mean." He twisted his head around and smiled.

Perry's skin heated as Simon's eyes scanned his face. He cleared his throat. "It would probably sell at auction for just under half a million."

Shooting up straight, the DS stared at Perry, his eyes wide open. "How much?"

Perry laughed. "I know. It's crazy money for a small clock. But not only is it made with gold and rose-cut diamonds, but every part is hand-crafted. The original would have taken about twelve months to make. You wouldn't believe how many specialists were involved. Not just the watchmaker but also the designer, the goldsmith who made the box, the enameller, the lapidary who cut, polished, and engraved the gems, the setter, and the engraver. It took an entire army of craftsmen to make each clock. It's a totally unique piece."

Shaking his head, Simon said, "Wow, I'd no idea. So I guess we don't need to ask what the motive was to steal it. How easy would it be to sell?"

Perry smiled. "A lot easier than you'd think. It's unlikely it would need to go to auction. There are several private collectors who would pay direct for something like this. And if it went through someone claiming to be a broker, they could plead confidentiality when selling. I suspect the buyer wouldn't ask too many questions."

"You know a lot about it. You're not the thief, are you?"

Perry gasped, all his breath knocked out of him. *Am I a suspect?* He'd never even thought about that possibility.

Reaching over, Simon touched his arm. "Breathe, Mr Juke." He chuckled. "I'm just kidding. I hardly think you'd have brought the swap to anyone's attention if you were."

Hands flying to his chest, Perry caught his breath. "That was mean," he mumbled.

Simon dropped his hand and looked down at his shoes. "I'm so sorry. It was just a joke. I didn't mean to upset you."

Perry giggled, and Simon looked up.

"Got you!" Perry crowed. Then, smiling, he said, "Please

call me Perry. And no, I'm not the thief. But I've worked here for nine years, so there isn't much I don't know about the rooms and their contents." He leaned towards Simon, lowering his voice. "And I can tell you, if I wanted to steal something from here, there is stuff worth a lot more than that clock." He winked at Simon and Simon laughed.

Retrieving an evidence bag and a pair of gloves, Simon picked up the clock. "I've agreed with Lady Sarah that we'll get this sent off to forensics straight away to see if they can lift off any fingerprints."

"I think that's unlikely. We all wear gloves to handle objects and furniture in the staterooms," Perry pointed out.

"I agree." Simon turned it over in his hand. "But they'll have a look, anyway. Then it'll be sent to our Specialist Fine Art division, where someone will confirm if it's the original or not. They may also shed some light on who might have been able to fake it." He slipped it into the bag and sealed it. "Right. Well, I've done as much as I can in here. If I remember rightly there's a nice restaurant on-site with a view of the main drive. Can we go there and a coffee? I'm parched."

# 7

## 11:20 AM, SATURDAY 8 JUNE

Perry placed a large black coffee in front of Simon and sat opposite him. "So what happens—"

"I bet you never get tired of this—"

They both laughed.

Perry nodded at Simon. "You go first."

"I was thinking that I'd never tire of this view."

They had found a table in the far corner of the Breakfast Room with a view of the Cascade — a magnificent water feature with two sets of stone steps, one facing south and the other facing north, over which water flowed from a set of fountains at the top.

"You're right. I find watching the water flow mesmerising. Did you know there are twenty-two steps on each side?"

"Yes. I counted them while you were getting our coffees."

Perry tilted his head to one side and grinned. "You didn't really, did you?"

His eyes shining, Simon grinned back. "No. I was texting Steve in the office to arrange for the clock to be picked up. You had a question?"

"Oh yes. So what happens next? Do we have to wait for it to be confirmed that it's definitely a fake?"

Simon shook his head. "No, as you and Lady Sarah are sure it's not the original clock, I'll carry on with the investigation on the basis that someone stole it and replaced it with a fake. It will take the art guys at least a few days to look at it anyway, and I don't want to wait that long. I doubt the thief expects we've discovered it this soon, so hopefully we'll have the advantage that he or she may not have disposed of the original yet or had time to cover all their tracks. We need to make the most of that. Assuming I believe you"—he looked at Perry, a wide grin across his face—"then we know you put the original clock back in the room on Thursday." He opened his notebook and, referring to it, continued, "At five thirty-one in the evening."

"How do you know the precise time? I'm impressed."

"Don't be. It's straightforward. That was the only time someone deactivated the room's alarm on Thursday. They reactivated it four minutes later. Anderson gave me a printout of the alarm records."

"There's a record of when someone switches the alarm on and off? I'd no idea."

He nodded. "It's a pretty common feature for this type of alarm."

"So does that mean…"

"Yes. The next time someone deactivated it was a quarter past six yesterday evening. They reactivated it five minutes later. That must be when the swap took place."

"I see. You're right. I'm not so impressed now." Perry grinned as he took a sip of his coffee.

"I told you. This detective stuff is really easy." Simon grinned back.

"So do you also have a theory about who did it? Oh, and before you say me again, I should tell you that Mrs Crammond, the head housekeeper, was with me the whole time the alarm was deactivated on Thursday. I don't have a key, so she had to be my escort."

"And there, you just hit the nail, or should I say the key, on the head. No, I don't know who it is yet, but all we need to know to narrow it down is to establish who has keys to the alarm—"

"And who was on site between six-fifteen and six-twenty yesterday!" Perry's eyes shined with excitement.

"Exactly." Simon nodded.

"So how do we do that?" Moving his coffee cup to the side, Perry pulled the plate with a chocolate brownie on it towards him. He cut it in half. "Help yourself," he said, pushing the plate with the remaining brownie across the table.

"Thanks." Simon took a bite, then flipped over a page of his notebook. "I've already had a list from Anderson of who has a set of alarm keys. They are: Lady Sarah Rosdale, Mrs Sophie Crammond, Mr Alistair Barnett, and Mr Marcus Crawley. Does that make sense to you?"

Perry nodded as he swallowed the last of his brownie and wiped his mouth with a napkin. "Yes, Lady Sarah oversees the management of the staterooms and all public areas. Mrs Crammond is the head housekeeper for all the public rooms. Alistair Barnett, also my boss, is the manager of the staterooms. And Marcus Crawley is the senior curator. He looks after all the collections here."

"Thanks. I've also found out which of these were off site on Friday at the critical time." He referred to his notebook again. "Mrs Crammond was logged leaving Francis Court via the north side gate at six thirty-four, so she is definitely on our list of suspects. I'll need to interview her to find out where she was and what she was doing."

Perry shook his head and guffawed. "Ah-ha! So that's how you knew it wasn't me; security must have logged me out before six-fifteen."

Raising his hands in front of himself, palms outwards, Simon conceded. "You've got me. They logged you out at six-thirteen."

*It's been a while since a man has made me laugh this much*, Perry thought. "What about the others?"

"Lady Sarah told me she left around four in the afternoon and went straight home to Francis Lodge. I have confirmed with her housekeeper that she arrived at four-fifteen and didn't go out again."

Perry nodded. "She has two youngish children who finish school at three-thirty. It's well known that she likes to be there when they get home."

"That rules Lady Sarah out. Security logged your boss, Barnett, out at six twenty-nine. He left in his car via the main gate."

"So it's not likely to be him either. He lives on-site in a flat in the Old Stable Block and I left him on his way there to pack." At Simon's curious look, he added, "His daughter is getting married today in Wales. He left to drive there last night." Perry shook his head. "He wouldn't have had time to get to his flat, pack, and get back in order to steal the clock at six-fifteen."

"So you saw him before you left?"

"Yes. I popped my head around his door at about six to tell him I'd locked up and was going home. We left his office together and parted ways at the bottom of the north terrace steps. He headed off to the Old Stable Block, and I walked to the north side gate which leads to the village."

Nodding, Simon said, "Well, if he went back to his flat when you left him, that would rule him out. I'll need to talk to him at some stage but as he's at a wedding today, it can wait until tomorrow. In the meantime, that just leaves—"

Perry raised his hand to his chest. "Marcus Crawley did it!"

# 8

## 11:40 AM, SATURDAY 8 JUNE

"Whoa, slow down, Sherlock. It's too early to say that. We have no evidence."

Perry's chair scraped along the floor as he jumped up. "We should interview him now."

Reaching forward as if to grab Perry's arm, Simon withdrew his hand and let it drop. "Wait," he said. "Anderson has already spoken to him."

Perry sat down again.

"Crawley claimed to have finished at five-thirty, then stayed in his flat all evening, watching TV. He said he didn't see anyone on the way to his flat and he didn't leave his flat once he was home."

"It's possible," Perry agreed. "Most of the household and staff finish as soon as the public leave, which at this time of year is at five. By five forty-five, it's often deserted. Especially where he lives in the Old Stable Block." He sighed and shook his head. "Anyway, surely it can't be him. He's been here for like a hundred years."

"Twenty, according to Anderson."

"It's a long time. I think he's too loyal to the family and the collection to do something like this."

"Possibly. But Anderson said he seemed nervous when he spoke to him, like maybe he was hiding something." Simon raised his eyebrows at Perry. "Look, I agree he isn't the most likely suspect, but he's currently without an alibi. I wish I could search his room and see if the clock was there."

"Why can't you?"

"I'd need a warrant. Him simply being on-site and having access to a key isn't enough to show probable cause for one."

"I could just ask him?" Perry suggested.

Simon's eyes lit up. "Do you think he'd say yes?"

"Can't hurt to ask."

---

Marcus Crawley opened the door of his apartment in the Old Stable Block, the quadrangle of flats and offices surrounding a courtyard attached at one end to the main house. His eyes, wrinkled at the corners, darted between Perry and Simon. "Hello. To what do I owe this pleasure?" he asked, scowling.

"I was wondering if we could have a word with you, Mr Crawley?" Perry said.

Crawley frowned. "Is this some sort of official visit?" He aimed his question at Simon.

"No, Mr Crawley, not at all," Perry answered for him. "It's just that DS Lattimore here wondered if he could have a look round your flat."

Crawley stood silently in his doorway. Perry thought he would turn them away.

"Does he think he will find the Cartier clock hidden in my underwear drawer?"

The side of his mouth quirking upwards, Perry replied,

"No, not at all, Mr Crawley." *Time to get tough with the old man.* "But if you let him have a quick look round now, it will be so much easier than him having to get a warrant and it appearing in the papers, don't you think?" He felt guilty when Crawley's face dropped and he grabbed onto the side of the door.

Perry reached his hand out, but Crawley shook his head.

"Okay, come in." Turning to Simon, the curator said, "You won't find anything, but I suppose you're only doing your job." Leaving the door open, he turned and shuffled back into his flat.

Although Perry had never been in any of the staff flats in the Old Stable Block before, he'd heard that they were very modern since being refurbished three years ago. So when Crawley led them into the sitting room, he'd not expected the high ceilings and the impressive picture windows. They immediately drew Perry to the view of the lake surrounded by woods that the flat afforded.

"It's a beautiful view you have here, Mr Crawley." Crawley, who was following Simon, turned and ambled back towards Perry.

"Yes. I think I've the best view of all the apartments here," he replied with pride. "The duchess picked it out for me personally, so I'm told."

Perry smiled, secretly doubting Princess Helen, the Duchess of Arnwall, would get involved in the allocation of staff flats. While known to be thoughtful and kind, Lady Sarah's mother would be too busy running Francis Court. He nodded anyway.

"Mr Barnett claims he has the better view next door, as he can see the long drive and the Cascade, but I love watching the deer as they move between the woods and the lake, so I think I win."

"Do you see much of Mr Barnett?" Perry asked, curious to know if his boss was as unsociable as he suspected.

"Not really. We both keep to ourselves. In fact, I hear him more than I see him."

Perry frowned. Crawley smiled. "These dividing walls are just plasterboard, so depending on what room you're in…" He shrugged. "I'm not complaining. Mr Barnett is normally quiet, and apart from days like yesterday, when he was banging around packing, we don't disturb each other much."

Laughing, Perry said, "Yes, I can't imagine he's a party animal." As he moved away from the window, he noticed Crawley's eyes darting towards the computer in the corner of the room. He recognised the logo flashing on the screen.

"So you play online poker, do you, Mr Crawley? A housemate of mine at university used that same site."

Red blotches appeared on Crawley's face. "Um, eh, I only dabble a bit, you know. Nothing serious."

Dropping onto the two-seater grey sofa, Perry leaned back and crossed his legs. "He did well out of it, from what I could tell. We only shared a house for a year, but he said it was enough to pay for his fees and accommodation."

Crawley eased himself into an armchair opposite. "Yes, well, if you're good, you can do all right."

Looking around the room, Perry recognised several paintings by moderately well-known modern artists and a display cabinet chock full of comic books. "And do you do all right with it, Mr Crawley?"

Crawley shifted forward in his chair and jutted out his chin. "I can't complain. It allows me to buy things I like." He glanced at the glass bookcase. "It may surprise you to know that I have little interest in antiques outside of work."

Smiling, Perry nodded. "Yes, I can see. I like your style, Mr Crawley."

Relaxing back into his chair, the older man looked delighted.

"So do you play in the evenings or on weekends?" Perry asked.

"Mostly in the evenings. The games at the weekend drag on too long for my liking."

Simon re-entered the living room. He caught sight of Perry and shook his head.

"And were you playing on Friday evening?" Perry asked.

Crawley peered at Simon. "Will this have to go any further? It's not something I'd like the duke and duchess knowing about."

Simon frowned. Turning, he looked over at Perry.

"Mr Crawley and I were just discussing online poker, sergeant. He likes to play sometimes."

Simon's face cleared, and he turned back to Crawley, shaking his head. "No, sir. If it has no relevance to the theft, then there's no need for it to go any further."

"Well, then yes, I was playing on Friday."

"What time?" Uncrossing his legs, Perry shifted forward in his seat.

"Well now, let me see." Crawley raised his hand to his face and stroked his chin. "I got home and made myself a sandwich. Then I signed in and waited until the next game was open. They normally open on the hour, so that would have made it a six o'clock start."

"And how long was your game, Mr Crawley?" Perry asked, his eyes shining.

"That one was just under an hour. Then I joined the next one but folded quickly. I called it a day after that. You have to know when to stop. I find that's the key to success."

"Yes. My friend used to say the same." Standing, Perry smiled at Crawley. "He had a handle. You know, like a nickname. It was the Cambridge Calculator, I think. He was reading maths."

Crawley smiled. "You can probably guess mine, Mr Juke. It's not very original."

"The Curator?"

"Not quite that literal." Crawley laughed. "It's the Keeper." He rose from his chair. "Would you gentleman like a cup of tea?"

"No, thank you, sir," Simon replied. "It's kind of you to offer, but I'm afraid we need to get on."

As they walked into the spacious corridor, Perry paused. "Sorry, Mr Crawley, just one last thing. You said you heard Mr Barnett banging around in his flat yesterday when he was packing. What time was that?"

"Well now, let me see. It was fifteen, maybe twenty minutes into my first game. I didn't hear much, just what sounded like something falling on the floor and then Mr Barnett coughing. He's getting over a nasty cold, I believe."

Perry glanced over at Simon, who raised his eyebrows. "Did you hear him arrive at his flat, sir?" Simon asked.

Crawley shook his head. "Although I did hear him leave as the door slammed shut."

"And what time was that?" Simon had taken his notebook out, his pen poised.

"About five minutes later." He leaned over and grabbed a piece of paper from a nearby sideboard. "In fact, he popped a note through the door as he left, apologising for making so much noise. He explained that his case had fallen out of the overhead cupboard." He pointed to a set of doors built into the wall above them. "You have to be careful what you store up there."

Perry and Simon nodded.

"Well, once again, thank you for your cooperation, Mr Crawley."

---

"What was that about online games?" Simon followed Perry across the Old Stable Block courtyard.

"Don't you see? He was playing poker online at the time of the theft. I know that site. They record the games played for later viewing. I think they use it for learning and teaching purposes or something. Mr Crawley had a webcam set up, so the chances are that your mate, Seb, in the office—"

"Do you mean Steve?"

"Yes, him. He should be able to find the game online and see the Keeper, aka Marcus Crawley, playing at the time the theft took place. And if he's lying, and he wasn't there, then he now thinks we don't suspect him."

Simon stopped on the cobbled ground and grabbed Perry's arm. "That's brilliant."

"As you said, it's easy this detecting thing."

Simon snorted, dropping Perry's arm. "And we also now have confirmation that Barnett went back to his room to pack and left around six twenty-five. So that puts him in the clear."

They stared at each other for a minute, grinning. Then Simon's smile disappeared. "You know what this means now, don't you?"

Perry nodded. "We only have one suspect left."

# 9

## 1 PM, SATURDAY 8 JUNE

"So what happens now?" Perry opened the drawer of his office desk and took out a tomato sauce sachet. He lifted it up and raised his eyes to Simon. Simon nodded and Perry slid it across the work top, then took another one out for himself.

Lifting the lid of his burger bun, Simon emptied the sachet on top of his patty before taking a huge bite. "We need to interview Mrs Crammond, but without her realising we know the clock is a fake," he replied, his voice muffled by a mouthful of food.

Perry, burger halfway to his face, nodded. After taking a bite, he used his napkin to wipe away the juices around his mouth. "Mmmm, this is so good."

They ate in companionable silence. They had almost finished when a head appeared around the door. "Hello, gentlemen. How are you getting on?"

Both men jumped to their feet, dropping food on the table in their rush to stand up.

"Please continue," Lady Sarah said. "I was just passing and wondered how things were going."

Sitting down again, Perry pushed his mostly eaten burger

to one side. "We're working through eliminating the list of suspects." *Well, that is true. Just don't ask for any more details*, he mentally begged her. He didn't want to be the one to tell her that her head housekeeper was currently their only suspect.

"That's fabulous. So how many do you have left?"

A flush of guilt crept up Perry's face. "Um, we're just—"

"We'd rather not discuss it at this stage, if you don't mind, my lady," Simon cut in. "It's a delicate stage in the investigation and the fewer people who know, the better."

Perry swallowed and smiled weakly at Simon. *Thanks for trying, but she'll never accept that.*

"Of course," she said, tapping the side of her nose. "Mum's the word. I'll leave you to it."

Simon gave Perry a grin of satisfaction as he popped the last piece of his burger into his mouth. "I needed that," he said as he wiped this mouth with a napkin. "Right, back to business." He threw the napkin and wrapper into the bin. "So what do we know about Mrs Crammond so far?" He retrieved his notebook from the back pocket of his trousers and opened it up. "We know she has access to the alarm keys and the room keys."

Perry nodded.

"We also know she was on-site at the time someone deactivated and reactivated the alarm."

Perry shot his hand up.

Simon paused. "Yes?"

"Quick question. We talked about motive and how it's most likely to be about money. But what I can't get my head around is why now? Mrs Crammond has been here for years. So why suddenly decide to do this now?"

Simon nodded. "That's a good question. Maybe she's having money troubles? What do you know about her?"

Leaning back in his chair, Perry crossed his arms. "Well, she was already at Francis Court when I first started, so that means she's been here for over nine years. She was assistant housekeeper then, working mainly in the family wing. She got a promotion a few years later and was housekeeper over at the Old Stable Block, looking after the flats and offices there. A couple of years ago, she moved to run the housekeeping staff looking after the state apartments and when Mrs Clarke, the head housekeeper, retired just under a year ago, they promoted her into the role. She lives in the village, near to me. I believe her mother has been ill recently and Mrs C moved her in with her so she could care for her."

"And what's she like as a person?" Simon asked.

"She's firm but fair with her staff, from what I hear. I've always found her very easy to work with. She's got a cheeky sense of humour, too." He shook his head. "I hope it's not her. She's really quite sweet..."

Simon inclined his head. "She may be, but she has a key, and she's the only one whose whereabouts at the time in question are unknown." His eyes softened as he leaned towards Perry. "She could have a legitimate reason. Maybe she accidentally broke it and is trying to cover it up while she gets it fixed?"

Perry nodded. That had to be it. "I guess we should go and talk to her."

---

Sophie Crammond was in her office, just a short stroll from Perry's, at her desk typing on her computer, when Perry and Simon arrived at her door.

"Mrs C, do you have a minute?" As Perry walked towards her desk, she got up to greet him.

"Yes, Perry. What can I do for you?" she asked him while fixing her gaze on Simon.

"This is DS Lattimore from Fenshire CID." Pulling out a chair opposite her, Perry sat down.

Rubbing the back of her neck with her left hand, she gestured towards the empty chair next to Perry with her right. "Please sit down, sergeant." As Simon sat down, she moved around the desk and closed the door. Returning to her chair, she cleared her throat. "How can I help you?"

*Is it my imagination or does she look twitchy?*

Perry smiled. "It's nothing to worry about, Mrs C. Mr Anderson has asked Fenshire CID to do a security review at Francis Court. You know what he's like, always wanting to make sure everything is in order."

Mrs Crammond nodded and leaned back in her chair, crossing her arms.

"So DS Lattimore here is doing some spot checks on security processes and in particular he's interested in talking to key holders." Perry looked over at Simon and nodded.

"Mrs Crammond, thank you for agreeing to talk to me. I won't take up much of your time," Simon said, smiling. Leaning forward, he retrieved his notebook from the back pocket of his trousers. "I understand you hold keys here in your office for the state rooms and their alarm systems. Is that correct?"

Uncrossing her arms, Mrs Crammond sat up straight. "Not quite, sergeant. I hold spare keys for all the staterooms. Mr Anderson, Mr Barnett, Lady Sarah, Mr Crawley, and Mr Juke permanently hold a full set. I am one of four alarm key holders, along with Lady Sarah, Mr Barnett, and Mr Crawley."

"Thank you for clarifying that, Mrs Crammond. And can I

ask you where you keep your keys when you are not using them?"

"Certainly, sergeant." She swivelled her chair around and pointed to the safe behind her desk. "I keep all the keys in here."

"And is that opened by an access code?" Simon asked.

She nodded and returned to face them.

"And who has the access code?"

"Just myself and Lady Sarah."

She started when her mobile phone vibrated in front of her. "I'm sorry, do you mind if I quickly take this?" she asked, grabbing the phone.

Simon and Perry shook their heads.

"Hello?" She rose from her desk and walked out of the office.

Perry jumped out of his chair and headed towards the door. Putting his finger up to his lips, he grinned at Simon. Poking his head around the open door, he saw Mrs Crammond halfway down the corridor, facing away from him. The wooden panelled walls, with their naturally sound-absorbing properties, meant he couldn't hear everything she said, but he got enough to get the gist of the conversation.

Darting back behind the door and hurrying to his seat, he just had time to whisper to Simon, "I'll tell you later," before Mrs Crammond walked back into the office.

"Sorry about that," she said as she resumed her seat. "Do continue, sergeant."

"Could you give me an example of your evening lock up process, please?"

"Well, first I check and lock up the Breakfast Room when the housekeeping team has finished cleaning. Then I walk around the Events Suite and make sure that is all in order and locked. When I've done all my checks, I let security know, and then I leave."

"So if we take yesterday as an example, what time was that, Mrs Crammond?"

"Well, yesterday we did a deep clean of the wooden floors in the Breakfast Room restaurant and the fridges in the attached kitchen, so it was probably about six o'clock before we finished and I locked up. Then I came back to my office to make a note of some cleaning materials I needed to order. After that, I checked all the rooms in the Events Suite were locked. I probably got back to my office about twenty past six. I rang security to tell them everything was checked and locked and then I left."

"Thank you, Mrs Crammond. And had everyone left for the day by then?"

She nodded. "I'm normally the last to leave, sergeant."

"Do you check the state apartments?"

Looking at Perry, she frowned. "No, Perry and Mr Barnett lock the staterooms."

"Quite right, Mrs C. I've already told the sergeant that, but he has to check as part of his review," Perry said, smiling.

"So, from about six onwards, you didn't see anyone?" Simon asked.

"I saw you, Perry, with Mr Barnett. I was in the Smoking Room returning some clean glasses and saw you outside through the French doors. Then, a little later, when I was in the Garden Room, I saw Mr Barnett go past the window. Apart from that, I didn't see anyone." She tilted her head to one side and gazed at Simon, her eyes narrowing. "Is something wrong, sergeant? Did something happen yesterday?"

Simon shook his head. "No, not at all, Mrs Crammond. I'm just trying to get an idea of the final security procedures on a typical day."

She scratched her left hand and looked away.

Simon rose. “Well, thank you for your help, Mrs Crammond. It seems like you have everything under control.”

Perry looked back as they walked to the door. Mrs Crammond’s chin was in her hands and she was staring at her phone.

---

“So what do you think about that?” Simon asked as they entered Perry’s office.

Sitting down behind his desk, Perry sighed and leaned back in his chair. “I don’t know. She seemed a bit agitated to me, which is unlike her. She’s normally calm and collected.”

“Could it have been something to do with the call she took?” Simon took his notebook out and plonked himself opposite.

“Oh, yes, the call. Of course. So I didn’t get all of it, but she definitely mentioned her mother. She said she would have the money in a few days and could they hold the room until then.”

“A care home?” Simon asked.

“Maybe.” Perry shrugged. “I guess if she stole the clock, that would explain why she now has the money…” He stared down at his hands and sighed.

“Look, I know you don’t want it to be her but unless you tell me she couldn’t have got from the Garden Room where she saw Barnett go past, to the Green Drawing Room in time to deactivate the alarm at six-fifteen, then she is still our only suspect.”

Looking up, Perry said, “So in five, maybe seven minutes tops?”

Simon nodded.

"It would be a push, but it would be possible if she really moved fast."

They sat in silence for a few minutes. Then Perry said, "But why would she go to the Events Suite in the first place if she was planning on swapping the clocks? Wouldn't she do that before, or maybe even after, she'd done her regular evening checks? Not halfway through. That makes no sense."

"That's a good point."

"Just out of curiosity, did security at the north side gate say if she was carrying anything when she left?" Perry leaned forward. "If she had the clock on her, it would be too big to go into her handbag."

Simon flipped through his notebook. He shook his head. "I have nothing noted here. Let me call them now." He reached over to the phone on Perry's desk and lifted the receiver. Perry dialled the number for him.

---

"Mrs C, sorry about the sergeant asking so many questions earlier. These security reviews are a real pain. Would you let me get you a coffee in the Breakfast Room to make up for it?" Perry said, smiling, his head craned around her office door.

"Well, that would be nice, Perry. I could do with a break." She rose and picked up her phone.

Following her along the corridor towards the back entrance of the restaurant, Perry glanced over his shoulder to see Simon sliding into her office.

---

"Well, this has been very pleasant, Perry," Mrs Crammond said as she stood and picked up her phone. "And thank you for letting me ramble on about the challenges of getting help with my mother."

Perry glanced at the door as he, too, stood up. *Where is Simon?* "I'm only sorry I couldn't be more help."

She smiled. "Sometimes, the only help you need is for someone to listen."

*She really is lovely. I hope he's not found anything.*

As Perry's eyes darted over Mrs Crammond's shoulder, Simon walked through the door. The tension left Perry's body, and smiling at her, he said, "Well, you know where I am if you ever need me."

---

"Well?" Perry picked up his second latte of the hour.

Simon shook his head. "Nothing."

"So we know she didn't take it off site, as security confirmed she didn't have a bag with her. And now we know the clock isn't in her office. Combined with the unlikeliness that she would start checking and locking the Events Suite, just to leave it halfway through to steal the clock, can we rule her out now?"

"Not so fast. We know she needs money, so she still has a motive. We can't disregard her completely, but I agree she's looking less likely as a suspect than she was before."

"So what now?" Perry asked, putting his cup down.

"We need to revisit our list of people who have alarm keys and review what we know about their opportunity and possible motive. If we've ruled everyone else out and it's not Mrs Crammond, then we must have missed something." He opened his notebook. "So first, Crawley. What do we know?

"I think we can rule Crawley out, pending Sam—"

"Steve," Simon cut in.

"Yes, him. Pending him getting back to us confirming Crawley's online presence. Oh, and I forgot to mention to you, did you see the things in his flat? He has tens of thousands of pounds worth of items on his walls and in his cabinet, and that was just the stuff we could see. He doesn't appear to be someone who needs money, so I don't see a motive either."

Simon nodded. "Yes, fair point. So next we have Lady Sarah. Her housekeeper confirms she was at home with her children from four-fifteen, so she is in the clear."

"Also," Perry added, "she's the daughter of a duke, the niece of the king, and is married to a wealthy investment broker. I can't see her needing money, either."

"Agreed. So that just leaves us with your boss, Alistair Barnett. What do you know about him?"

"Not much, really. He's been my boss for less than a year and he's not particularly sociable. His wife died four, maybe five, years ago. They lived in the village, but after her death he moved on-site. He has just the one child — the daughter getting married today."

"How old is he?"

"I don't know, maybe mid-fifties?" Perry picked up his phone. "Claire will know," he said as he typed a text message. "But does it really matter?" he asked as he pressed send. "Crawley heard Barnett next door at the time of the theft, so surely that rules him out, too?"

Simon sighed and nodded slowly.

Perry huffed. "Anyway, they've all been here for years. So why now? And why the clock? There are more valuable pieces to steal if you really needed a large amount of money urgently. It just makes no sense to me."

"Could we have missed anyone?" Simon asked.

Perry shrugged. They sat in silence while Simon flipped through the pages of his pocketbook.

*This is so frustrating! Someone has done it, but who and why?* Perry straightened up as excitement rose in his chest. "Oh my giddy aunt, I've got it!" He froze when Simon snorted. "What?" he asked.

"Oh my *what*?" Simon's face crinkled, his eyes shining.

Heat rode up Perry's neck. "Oh my giddy aunt. You must have heard someone say that before?"

"Er, no," Simon choked.

As Simon continued to laugh, Perry frowned. *Why is he laughing at me?* He wanted to be mad at him over being teased, instead couldn't help but think how endearing the sergeant looked wiping a tear from his eye.

"I'm sorry," Simon said, taking a deep breath and grinning. "I've just never heard that phrase before today."

*I must stop overreacting!* Perry grinned back.

"Anyway, you were saying?" Simon continued.

Perry's face lit up. "What if this isn't the first time the thief has stolen something?"

# 10

## 1:30 PM, SATURDAY 8 JUNE

Roisin: *No fingerprints on the fake clock. Arts department still determining if it's a fake.*

Steve: *Crawley is in the clear. The Keeper is visible throughout the game which started at 18:00 and ended at 18:57.*

---

Simon put his phone down on Perry's office desk. "So you're suggesting that someone has been swapping out items for years and never been caught?" His eyes were wide. "Surely there are checks done regularly? Don't items have to be cleaned or repaired? Wouldn't it get spotted then? And anyway, wouldn't the curator be the one dealing with items that were being moved?"

"Well, that's the thing." Perry leaned forward, placing his palms on the desk. "Three years ago, Crawley was at Kilkirk House in Ireland — it's one of the Duke's other properties —

doing an inventory. He was only supposed to be there for a week or so, but he had a fall and broke his leg. He ended up being there for four months."

His phone pinged.

Claire: *Barnett is 59. In fact he's due to retire in ten weeks. Why do you need to know? And who is the gorgeous man you stood me up for? News travels fast… x*

He smiled. *Simon* is *gorgeous.* And Perry was about to impress him… he hoped.

"During that time, Barnett took over the moving of objects around the state rooms, as well as their removal for cleaning and repair. When Crawley got back, they decided that the arrangement had worked so well that they'd continue it. I know there's some double checking in place, but I don't know what it is. We'll need to ask Crawley."

---

Perry was studying the catalogue of items when Crawley stepped into his office. Perry rose. "Mr Crawley, thank you for responding so promptly to our request for some help. I hope we're not disturbing your day off any more than we have already?"

Smiling, Crawley replied, "It's all right, Mr Juke. I needed a break anyway, and I'm happy to help."

Simon walked into the room, carrying two takeaway coffee cups. He handed one to Perry. "Ah, Mr Crawley. Thank you for coming. Would you like a drink?"

"No thank you, sergeant. I've drunk enough coffee

already today to keep me on the go until this evening. Now what can I do for you, gentlemen?"

Simon looked over at Perry and nodded.

"We have been looking at the catalogue." Perry gestured at his computer. "And we have a couple of questions about procedures, if that's all right?"

Crawley nodded.

"For the last three years Mr Barnett is the one who organises items to be cleaned, repaired, and returned. Is that correct?"

"Yes. When I was indisposed by a fall at Kilkirk House, it worked well. So when he suggested we continue the arrangement, I was happy to agree. It saved me a job, and really, it made more sense for him to do it as he was looking after the displays. It also allowed us to add an extra layer of security."

"How do you mean?" Simon asked.

"Me and my team took over the audits and checks to assess when items needed to be cleaned or repaired. Previously, that decision had been left solely to Mr Barnett."

Simon frowned. "I'm sorry, but I'm not following."

"With him taking over the arrangements to get the work done, we could set up biannual audits where my team examined items and determined if they needed cleaning or repair. What do you youngsters call it? Proactive management?" He chuckled.

Perry's enthusiasm waned. He cringed. *I'm going to look like a fool.* If there were biannual checks for everything, there was no way anyone would've been able to steal multiple pieces without being caught.

"I see. So as far as you're concerned, your team see all items at least twice a year?" Simon asked.

Crawley nodded.

Perry swallowed. Crawley's team were well respected too. *Surely they would notice if an item was a fake.*

"And would they have noticed if an item was a fake?" Simon asked.

Crawley's eyes widened. "Yes, sergeant. My team is very experienced. I would be surprised if they missed something like that. We do a thorough examination."

"Yes, thank you, Mr Crawley. I'm sure you do." Simon looked at Perry and shook his head subtly.

Sitting down and staring at his screen, Perry took the time to smother his disappointment. He'd been so sure he was on to something. But then, even if he was, Barnett had an alibi for the time of the theft, still leaving only Mrs Crammond as the possible thief. Could she have been stealing valuable objects under the nose of those two men? *That isn't possible... is it?*

His eyes rested on a line in the catalogue featuring a hand-painted Sèvres porcelain parrot vase circa 1925. *I remember that.* Quite garish, with a big blue parrot on it, the vase used to sit on the oversized console table in the Green Drawing Room. It hadn't been there for a good few months, though. Running his eyes across the screen, he was excited to see what he found.

"Mr Crawley." When the man turned to look at him, Perry beckoned him over and pointed to the entry in the database. "This Sèvres porcelain parrot vase. Do you remember it?"

Taking out his glasses and leaning over Perry's shoulder, Crawley nodded. "Yes. It isn't the most attractive object. Despite that, it's worth at least ninety-thousand pounds."

"According to this, Mr Barnett removed it for cleaning back in March." Perry moved his finger horizontally along the screen. "But rather than it being put back on display when it was returned in April, it's marked down as in storage. So what happens then?"

Crawley straightened up. "It would stay there until someone needed it again for a display and then it would be checked in the same way we have previously discussed."

"But what happens if it stays in storage?" Simon interrupted. He was looking at Perry, his eyes shining.

*He's got it now*, Perry thought.

"Is there an audit or review of items in storage?"

Crawley nodded. "Yes, we do a biannual stock take."

Tilting his head slightly, Simon frowned and looked over at Perry.

Perry shared Simon's look of concern. "When you say stock take, Mr Crawley… what does that involve?" he asked.

"We go to each location and make sure the item there is the same as in the catalogue and that it agrees with our list of items in stock."

"So you're just checking that they are there? You're not doing a physical examination of them?" Perry held his breath. *Please let this be the answer I want.* He crossed his fingers underneath his desk.

Crawley shook his head. "No, there's no need. We keep each item in our storage rooms inside a glass box, some of which are temperature controlled. We switch all working parts off. They are clean and safe there. We don't want to disturb them or risk them being damaged by taking them out of the boxes, so we do a visual check, then we scan the tags on the boxes and match them to the database."

Uncrossing his fingers, Perry leaned back in his chair and grinned at Simon.

"Mr Crawley, can you do me a favour, please?" Simon gestured towards the door. "Can you accompany me to where you store the items and examine some of them for me? I would value your opinion."

Crawley looked between the two men, a frown on his face. "Of course, if you think it would be helpful."

"It will be *very* helpful, Mr Crawley," Simon said, as he held his arm out to guide the man through the door. Following him, Simon turned around and, grinning, he gave Perry a thumbs up.

---

"How long do you think it will take him?" Picking up his fourth coffee of the afternoon from the table in front of him in the Breakfast Room, Perry took a sip. *Maybe I need to switch to tea.*

Simon shrugged. "If the first three he examined are anything to go by, it could take all day. He was calling in two of his team to help when I left."

"Do you think any of them are fakes?"

"Crawley has confirmed nothing yet, but judging by the look on his face, the second and third items — a decorative egg and a miniature glass horse — weren't the originals either. He was quite upset when he was on the phone with his team."

"I wonder how many items have been stolen." Perry put his cup down and shook his head. "I just can't see Mrs Crammond being the mastermind behind this. How would she swap out objects without Barnett or Crawley being aware? And does she really have the contacts to get such good fakes made, let alone sell the originals? It seems so unlikely."

"But if it's not her, then who is it? Crawley and Barnett have alibis, remember?"

Perry took a deep sigh and grabbed one of the two pain au

chocolat on the plate in front of him. He took a bite. Mrs Crammond being the thief felt wrong. *What am I missing?* He frowned. *There's something, I'm sure. But what is it?* Looking over to the restaurant serving counter, he caught sight of Flo, now in a coat, walking out from behind it. She saw him and waved. "See you Tuesday," she shouted across the room.

*Tuesday? Why not Monday?* He frowned before shaking his head. Oh, of course, he was normally off on a Monday. She wouldn't know he'd swapped his day off, as one of his team wanted a long weekend away.

As he waved Flo off, his frown returned.

*But Barnett knew I had swapped my day off, so why did he say, 'See you Tuesday.'?*

Lost in thought, it startled Perry when Lady Sarah suddenly appeared at their table.

"Are you gentlemen *still* drinking coffee?" she asked, grinning.

Perry crossed his arms. "Actually, we've been very busy since we last saw you," Perry informed her.

"So do you know who the thief is yet?"

Perry caught Simon's eye. Simon shook his head.

"We currently have a solid working theory, my lady, but we still have a few things to sort out before I can disclose the information. I'm sure you understand," Simon replied.

Smiling, she nodded at Simon.

*How does he do that?* Perry shook his head. *She's a pussycat with him.*

Still mulling over why Barnett had forgotten about him working on Monday, Perry asked, "Lady Sarah, is Mr Barnett out on Monday? I'm not aware he's booked a day off but he may have forgotten to tell me."

She nodded. "Yes. It was all very last minute. He only asked me late Friday afternoon. He said something about an appointment in London. Right, I must get on. Please let me know when you have something definite."

"What was that about?" Simon asked, as they watched Lady Sarah glide out of the room.

"The last thing Barnett said to me yesterday was, 'See you Tuesday', but he knew I was due to work on Monday. That could only mean that he was the one who wouldn't be here on Monday."

Simon frowned. "I don't see the relevance. Maybe he's just making a long weekend of it."

"You're probably right." Perry placed his elbows on the table and rested his chin on his hands.

"What is it?" Simon asked as he picked up the remaining pastry.

"I know this will sound silly, but I've a bad feeling about Barnett." Perry raised his hand towards Simon. "Before you tell me, I know he has an alibi. But something is bugging me and I can't pull it from my brain."

Picking up a napkin, Simon wiped his mouth. "Okay. Let's go back to the last time you saw him. Start with when you went into his office before you left on Friday."

Perry put his hands up to his forehead and leaned into them. *Think*! He tried to picture the scene in his mind. "Keys!" he cried.

Simon, who had been drinking his coffee, placed it down and picked up his pen. "Keys?"

"Yes. There was a small bunch of keys on his desk when I walked in. As he was talking to me, he swept them into his top drawer. Later, just before we left his office, he took something out of the same drawer and put it in his jacket pocket."

"The alarm keys?"

"Could be. I've only seen Mrs Crammond's set, but they looked similar in size."

"Anything else?"

Perry clapped his hands together. "Yes! There was a small leather bag on the floor, which he picked up as we left. It was about the right size to contain the clock. Do you think he had the fake in there ready to swap out?"

"Could be," Simon said, making a note in his pocketbook.

"But his alibi—" Perry stopped when he saw Claire hurrying across the restaurant towards them, a glint in her eye.

"Hello," she said, staring at Simon, making no effort to disguise her interest. She shifted her gaze to Perry and not so subtly nodded her head sideways in Simon's direction.

Perry laughed. "Claire, this is Detective Sergeant Lattimore. He's here doing a security review for Mr Anderson. Sergeant, this is Claire Beck. Claire works in HR."

"Please call me Simon," Simon said as he held his hand out.

"You look familiar," Claire said as she shook it.

"DS Lattimore was part of the investigation team working on the Earl of Rossex's death, so he's been here before."

Claire raised her eyebrows at Perry as she sat down. Putting her elbows on the table and pressing her hands together, she said, "So, Simon, are we all safe and sound here at Francis Court?"

"Erm, yes, from what I can see," Simon replied.

Perry looked at his watch. *Claire, I love you, but please go.* Perry wanted to carry on discussing Barnett with Simon. *I think we have something.* "I thought you'd be gone by now. Don't you finish at one?" he asked her.

"Yes, normally. But I wanted to stay and finish some filing. So why were you asking how old Barnett is?"

"No reason, just curious." Perry could feel his colour rising. Claire glared at him. *She doesn't believe me.* He needed to distract her.

"I wonder how his daughter's wedding is going? I think the ceremony was at two, so they should be married by now."

"I hope it went well." Claire smiled, then shook her head. "He looked so flustered when I saw him packing his car yesterday afternoon. He dropped his suit carrier while he was getting all his stuff into the boot."

Simon shot a look at Perry. "What time was that, Claire?" Simon asked, his eyes shining.

"Oh, about half past four, I guess. Why?"

"No reason, just curious." Simon grinned at Perry.

"Well, you are a pair of curious Georges," she said, looking from one to the other, smirking. Her gaze rested on Perry, her eyes wide. After a few minutes of getting no response, she rose.

"Well, nice to meet you, Simon. Perry, I'll ring you later," she said, her face telling him he could expect a long call.

After watching her strut out of the room, Perry turned to Simon. "Oh my giddy aunt! Does that mean what I think it means?"

Simon nodded. "Barnett had already packed his bags and loaded his car before the theft. He didn't need to go back to his flat." He shook his head. "I don't know how he convinced Crawley that he was there packing, but I think he doubled back after he left you and swapped the clock—"

"Putting it in the small leather bag he was carrying!" Perry cried. "Do you think he is going to London to—"

"Get rid of the clock?" Simon finished for him. Picking up his phone, he dialled his office.

# 11

# 10 AM, SUNDAY 9 JUNE

Simon: *Barnett arrested at 9:00 this morning. Clock found in a small leather bag in the boot of his car.*

Perry: *Thanks for letting me know. How is Wales?*

Simon: *Wet and cold!*

Perry: *How is Barnett?*

Simon: *Initially surprised, tried to bluff it out. It shook him when we found the clock. He claimed someone must have planted it on him. We can hold him for 24 hours. By then Crawley should have completed his assessment and Barnett will struggle to get out of it.*

Perry: *Let me know how it goes and try not to drown or get hypothermia.*

---

Lady Sarah: *They have arrested Barnett. DS Lattimore has insisted that he couldn't have done it without you. Ma & Pa are thrilled and they want to thank you in person. Will you have lunch with them on Friday?*

*Oh my giddy aunt.* Lunch with the Duke of Arnwall and Her Royal Highness Princess Helen. *Wait until I tell Claire about this...*

# 12

## MID-MORNING, TUESDAY 20 AUGUST

"Hello, stranger." Perry grinned at a sun-kissed Simon Lattimore standing in his office doorway. "You look well."

Grinning back, Simon walked in and stopped in front of Perry's desk. Perry rose and held his hand out. Simon shook it firmly.

"I've been on holiday. But now that I'm back, I've just had the pleasure of returning the Cartier mystery clock to Lady Sarah. She seemed pleased."

"The whole family couldn't wait to get it back. It's not just that it's valuable, but it was Evelyn's favourite. They want to put it back in the room next to her picture, where it belongs. What happens to the fake one?"

"Our art guys have to keep that as evidence. They'll need it to prosecute Barnett's partner in crime, Joseph Timms. He's already known to them, but they had nothing substantial to charge him with until now. They're over the moon." A huge grin spread across his face.

*His teeth look so white against his tan.* He looked even more dreamy than Perry remembered.

"And how is Barnett?"

"Once he accepted we'd caught him red-handed, he caved in and did a deal to shop in Timms. He'll give evidence against him when it goes to trial and in return he'll get a reduced sentence, probably in an open prison. They're still working out a value for the fifteen items he swapped out over the last three years, but whatever it is, he'll have to pay it back. He was saving it for his retirement. Apparently, he was planning to go off to live in Thailand."

"Who would've thought it?" Perry said, shaking his head. "I still can't believe he'd got away with it for so long. He had some neck."

Grinning like the Cheshire Cat, Simon said, "Well, he was most adamant that if it hadn't been for you, he *would* have got away with it."

Perry raised his hand to his chest. "Me? What did I do?"

"You returned the clock to the Green Drawing Room while he was off work with that bad cold." When Perry frowned, Simon continued, "He already had a buyer for the clock, who was leaving town on the Tuesday. His plan was to keep the clock back after it was returned from cleaning and put the fake into storage, as he'd done so successfully before. But because you put it back on display, he then had to do the swap. He knew unless he left the fake in its place, you'd spot its absence when you were doing your staff training and start asking questions. He'd planned to replace it with another item when he returned on Tuesday, but of course by then it was too late."

"Wow." Perry shook his head. "So did you find out how he convinced Crawley he was packing in his flat when he was actually stealing the clock?"

Simon nodded. "Barnett went back to his apartment at lunchtime that day and recorded the sound of him getting out his case and dropping it. Then he used his phone to play it via his laptop in the flat while he doubled back and did the swap. Afterwards he rushed to his flat via the south side door, went in quietly, and turned off his computer. When he left, he banged the door loudly so Crawley could hear it. He then popped the note through Crawley's letterbox to apologise for the noise, hoping that it would reiterate to Crawley that he'd been there all along."

"Clever," Perry said. "And he admitted all this, did he?"

"Yes. He was very keen to tell us just how smart he'd been. Although… there was a witness who saw him going back towards the north side door after you and he had parted. We just didn't pick up on it when they told us." He tilted his head to one side and cocked his eyebrow at Perry.

"Mrs Crammond!" Perry cried. "She told us she saw Barnett go past the Garden Room window, but we didn't ask her in which direction he was going."

Simon nodded and smiled. "Full marks, Sherlock."

They stared at each other for a few minutes, smiling, before Perry broke the silence. "Do you have time for a coffee?"

Simon grinned. "I always have time for a coffee."

*The End*

I hope you enjoyed *Tick, Tock, Mystery Clock*. If you did then please consider writing a review on Amazon or Goodreads, or even both. It helps me a lot if you let people know that you recommend it.

. . .

**Want to see more of Perry and Simon?** Want to hear more about life (and death) at Francis Court? Find out in *Spruced up for Murder* the first in the A Right Royal Cozy Investigation series available in Amazon or wherever you get your paperback books from. **You can read chapter one on the next page.**

For other books in the series take a look at the back of this book.

If you want to find out more about what I'm up to you can find me on Facebook at helengoldenauthor , Instagram at helengolden_author and TikTok at @helengoldenauthor.

**Be the first to know when my next book is available.** Follow Helen Golden on Amazon, Bookbub, and Goodreads to get alerts whenever I have a new release, preorder, or a discount on any of my books.

# CHAPTER 1 — SPRUCED UP FOR MURDER

**Early morning, Wednesday 7 April**

"Oh my giddy aunt!" Perry Juke slapped his hand up to his mouth, his face turning pale as he gawped at the body in front of them.

"Oh my giddy aunt, indeed," Lady Beatrice, the Countess of Rossex, replied, gazing at the prone form lying only a few metres away from her. Her stomach twisted at the sight of his lifeless body. Instinctively, she wanted to look away, but like a moth attracted to a light, she was drawn to the scene before her.

He — for it was definitely a man with his stocky frame and shaved head — was lying on his front, his arms and legs splayed out, looking rather like he had fallen from a great height. Blood obscured the right-hand side of his face. A patch of what looked like red wine had soaked into the green and black Persian rug underneath his body. The grey marble table, which was normally by the side of the olive-green leather Chesterfield, was lying askew on the floor. One corner was covered in something dark and sticky.

"He must have fallen and hit his head on the table. Is he

dead? He looks very dead," Perry said, scanning the room as if searching for someone to confirm the body was, indeed, dead.

Lady Beatrice raised her hand to her chest to still her racing heart.

*The press is going to love this.*

A dead body at Francis Court, found by a member of the royal family — this was gold.

She raked her slim fingers through her long auburn hair. If only she hadn't been guilted by her mother into accepting her sister's request to take on the interior design of the refurbished Events Suite, she would be upstairs in her apartment right now, enjoying a leisurely coffee and snuggling with her dog, Daisy. Shaking her head, she returned to the matter in hand. There was possibly a dead body in front of them, and it had to be dealt with.

*I suppose one of us needs to check for a pulse.*

She turned hopefully to Perry.

To Read more, order your copy of *Spruced Up For Murder* now.

## A BIG THANK YOU TO...

I would like to mention a few people who helped and supported me in the writing of this short story.

First, I must thank my lovely husband Simon, who was unwavering in his support and generously dragged me out of the caravan every few weeks so he could clean it.

To my fabulous stepdaughter Ellie, who popped in to check on me regularly and reminded me I needed to take some time out… by watching TV with her.

To my best girl Emma, for checking in with me frequently and providing Bourbon for company.

To my parents Ann and Ray, for your feedback on my first draft and for helping me come up with a better title. Thank you.

To my beta readers, Lesley Catterall-Price and Peter Boon, as always, your feedback has been invaluable.

To my editor, Marina Grout, who simply makes everything sound better, and to Georgiana Hockin, my great friend who proofread this for me. Thank you both for your support and encouragement. You are both a pleasure to work with.

To my lovely friend Carolyn Bruce for being my final eyes, although any mistakes are, of course, totally my responsibility.

To you, my readers, thank you for signing up to my author group. I hope you enjoyed meeting Simon and Perry, and that we can continue to enjoy them and my other characters together as the Lady Beatrice series unfolds.

And finally, thank you to my wonderful companions — Alfie, Margot, and occasionally, Bourbon. Your (mostly) calm presence was a comfort as I have sat, head in hands, trying to write something worth reading.

I may have taken a little dramatic license when it comes to police procedures, so any mistakes or misinterpretations, unintentional or otherwise, are my own.

# CHARACTERS IN ORDER OF APPEARANCE

## TICK, TOCK, MYSTERY CLOCK

**Perry Juke** — head tour guide at Francis Court.

**Alistair Barnett** — Manager of the state rooms at Francis Court. Perry's boss.

**Frank** — security officer at Francis Court.

**Flo** — server in the Breakfast Room at Francis Court.

**Claire Beck** — Perry's friend who works in human resources at Francis Court.

**Colin** — would-be guide at Francis Court.

**Lady Sarah Rosdale** — manager of staterooms and public areas, Francis Court. Daughter of Charles Astley and HRH Princess Helen. Granddaughter of present king.

**Charles Astley** — Duke of Arnwall. Owner of Francis Court.

**Her Royal Highness Princess Helen** — Duchess of Arnwall. Daughter of the current king.

**Marcus Crawley** — senior curator at Francis Court

**Jack Anderson** — Francis Court's head of security.

**Simon Lattimore** — detective sergeant, Fenshire CID.

**Mrs Sophie Crammond** — head housekeeper of public rooms at Francis Court.

**Steve** — detective sergeant, Fenshire CID.

**Roisin** — Simon's best friend who works in Forensics, Fenshire Police.

# ALSO BY HELEN GOLDEN

A short prequel in the series A Right Royal Cozy Investigation. Can Perry Juke and Simon Lattimore work together to solve the mystery of the missing clock before the thief disappears? FREE novelette when you sign up to my readers' club. See end of final chapter for details. Ebook only.

First book in the A Right Royal Cozy Investigation series. Amateur sleuth, Lady Beatrice, must pit her wits against Detective Chief Inspector Richard Fitzwilliam to prove her sister innocent of murder. With the help of her clever dog, her flamboyant co-interior designer and his ex-police partner, can she find the killer before him, or will she make a fool of herself?

Second book in the A Right Royal Cozy Investigation series. Amateur sleuth, Lady Beatrice, must once again go up against DCI Fitzwilliam to find a killer. With the help of Daisy, her clever companion, and her two best friends, Perry and Simon, can she catch the culprit before her childhood friend's wedding is ruined?

The third book in the A Right Royal Cozy Investigation series. When DCI Richard Fitzwilliam gets it into his head that Lady Beatrice's new beau Seb is guilty of murder, can the amateur sleuth, along with the help of Daisy, her clever westie, and her best friends Perry and Simon, find the real killer before Fitzwilliam goes ahead and arrests Seb?

A Prequel in the A Right Royal Cozy Investigation series. When Lady Beatrice's husband James Wiltshire dies in a car crash along with the wife of a member of staff, there are questions to be answered. Why haven't the occupants of two cars seen in the accident area come forward? And what is the secret James had been keeping from her?

ALL EBOOKS AVAILABLE IN THE AMAZON STORE.

PAPERBACKS AVAILABLE FROM WHEREVER YOU BUY YOUR BOOKS.

# ALSO BY HELEN GOLDEN

When the dead body of the event's planner is found at the staff ball that Lady Beatrice is hosting at Francis Court, the amateur sleuth, with help from her clever dog Daisy and best friend Perry, must catch the killer before the partygoers find out and New Year's Eve is ruined.

Snow descends on Drew Castle in Scotland cutting the castle off and forcing Lady Beatrice along with Daisy her clever dog, and her best friends Perry and Simon to cooperate with boorish DCI Fitzwilliam to catch a killer before they strike again.

A murder at Gollingham Palace sparks a hunt to find the killer. For once, Lady Beatrice is happy to let DCI Richard Fitzwilliam get on with it. But when information comes to light that indicates it could be linked to her husband's car accident fifteen years ago, she is compelled to get involved. Will she finally find out the truth behind James's tragic death?

An unforgettable bachelor weekend for Perry filled with luxury, laughter, and an unexpected death.
Can Bea, Perry, and his hen's catch the killer before the weekend is over?

Bake Off Wars is being filmed on site at Francis Court and everyone is buzzing. But when much-loved pastry chef and judge, Vera Bolt, is found dead on set, can Bea, with the help of her best friend Perry, his husband Simon, and her cute little terrier, Daisy, expose the killer before the show is over?

ALL EBOOKS AVAILABLE IN THE AMAZON STORE.

PAPERBACKS AVAILABLE FROM WHEREVER YOU BUY YOUR BOOKS.

Made in the USA
Columbia, SC
30 June 2024

37919879R00050